BRICKS

A *These Americans* Novella

Aaron Paul Schaut

"Words from that trumpet of the morning
in America, Emerson, he who announced
Whitman and also said 'Infancy conforms to
nobody' —infancy of the simplicity of just being
happy in the woods, conforming to nobody's
idea about what to do, what should be done."

— Jack Kerouac, Big Sur

reminders.

Routine

It's dark out. — Even in a Lucid dream such as this, one might find this darkness rather cliché. However many times it's been said, it would be a shame to not unpack this three-word introduction for the fact that it's evening. — So, even though there are no windows in this room, I can feel in both my fingertips and spine that the earth has escaped the sun during this final transition from day to night — this final transition before a particular set of crimes. I can smell the booze and the crack pipes wafting off the lips of the city's college crowd, the city's hookers, and the city's whores. Far be it from me to judge a student or a sex worker or whomever or whatever the reader. On this night, I can feel the tug of murder — the barely audible last breath is fogging the cosmic mirror: the body's resonance, the blood smell in the air. The essence of death has followed this night's gentle and warm breeze between the houses and buildings and streetlights. Death has traveled between the drunk and sleeping homeless, perched up against the brick walls and doorways, and through the walls and ducts and vents of One Monroe, Police Plaza, and into my gut's sinus cavity.

It's past that time of night that everyone in the building has clocked out but me. For me, it's time to go to work — time to get things done — for me, the night offers the overtime, and I'm taking the work — need it. For me, the work is always guaranteed.

I wake up hard and light up a smoke. Why not? The hell with it. I look at the clock; it's 4 am, almost time for my morning jog. I'll stand at my bedside and stare at my reflection in the window. I wonder if I'm still in my dream or if my awareness of routine is in fact, a fact. The sheets are warm and damp, and my alarm is repeating its obnoxious and extreme "Brap, Brap, Brap" rant.

I've had this noir fucking dream, or variations of it, for as long as I can remember, disappointed that I never get to the part with a dame. Maybe someday she will show up in an epilogue to this recurring night. I know the dame is there, somewhere in the deep recesses of my brain. She's mysterious and elusive, waiting for the right time to make an appearance. I'm afraid for it to happen. She might be Death — she might be all dolled up for my funeral, a cop's funeral, just like Dad's funeral. Maybe she's not Death at all. Maybe she's never gonna show her face. Maybe, this whole time, it's just me, waiting for the hunt but never getting it, never satisfied and always reeling.

Opening the door for my morning jog, I'm greeted by this cat they call Gilbert and a cold can of Coke that is always left sitting on my front porch. The cat only shows up because I feed him — the Coke is somewhat of a mystery to me. I get the feeling that my neighbor Victoria sets it out for me. She's the type to do that sort of thing — support the boys in blue and all. She's attractive enough, but what do I know about attractive?

This morning's air is damp or humid and smells like wet grass and ripe leaves and cinnamon from the bread factory that sits next to the jail up the street — yes, I'm in close proximity to the jail. That strange round building housing all those case files, stuffed into those walls with little rectangular windows. It's merely a car alarm's audible distance from my house. Every once in a while, a transferee books (as opposed to being booked), cuffs and all, on foot across the field and train tracks and highway and into my neighborhood. A scurry of squad cars and badges roll around and walk around until they find their runaway. The runaway is usually tucked under somebody's RV or in somebody's boat or shed, realizing that it's only a matter of time before they'll get found. They hear the dogs and the chirps of the sirens and the distant voices of the officers replying to the distorted speech and beeps coming from their radios. This is just a thing that happens every once and a while. It can be entertaining. The runner was usually a possession charge and posed little threat to the community.

It's mid-summer and these last few days have hit ninety degrees and the suit and tie only amplify the heat. No, I won't tone down my attire for the weather. Uncomfortable as it might be a good detective has got to look the part. In my suit and in my tie, I place the Coke and my mug of coffee into the GTO's over-the-hump cup holders that drape around the 4-speed stick. I'll leave the Bonneville at home today. It's too nice out for a stuffy ride — gotta look the part.

The drive to work always finds me admiring a lot of leftovers from the previous night's debauchery. Takes me back to my time as a beat cop, strolling up and down these streets poking at the leftover riff-raff. The sidewalks on this particular west side street are still littered with half-empty pint glasses and plastic shot bottles, empty cups, random used rubbers, and the late risers still sleeping in doorways. Some of these heavy sleepers are homeless, others simply didn't make it home.

Passing Luke's Lanes, a fifty-some-year-old bowling alley, I throw a low wave, just barely bringing my hand off the car window's edge, toward officers John Sanchez and Emmitt Round. These two beat cops are sitting in their squad car in the bowling alley's blacktop parking lot, drinking coffee and getting ready to remove the unwanted from their makeshift sleeping quarters. I remember sitting in that same parking lot in my GRPD squad car.

Crime has been ramping up with the heat. It's human nature. High heat leads to an increased heart rate — which makes people uncomfortable. This agitation leads to anger and the anger leads to violence, or so they tell me — or so Annie tells me. Try walking a beat in ninety-degree weather in full uniform and keeping your cool — a layer of grease and sweat between you and your uniform while your pants are chaffing up the inside of your thighs, all while you're getting an earful of shit-talk from some fucking dealer or a prostitute or a disgruntled somebody-anybody. You have to constantly remind yourself that your firearm is not on your hip as a tool for stress relief.

Entering One Monroe (not as sexy as it sounds) at 8 o'clock in the morning finds me reading the introduction to the day's violence. I'm on page one, and I'm the editor and my goddamn white-out pen is empty.

"Morning John," Officer Ryan sits behind the reception desk in the atrium of One Monroe.

"Morning, Ryan. How'd last night play out for you? It's hot out there."

Though only paying a modicum of attention, I heard Ryan's list. The night saw several car thefts, a slew of domestic violence calls, some houses and cars were shot up at random, and several businesses were broken into. Maybe I heard Ryan mutter this list. Maybe I'd heard the same list in my head every time I'd asked this question.

"So, another busy night then?"

"Yes, sir," Ryan replied. "Job security."

"Maybe. See you later, Ryan."

I dressed my desk with a case folder full of missing guys. I've been working on these missing persons cases for nearly a year and always come up short of leads. I take a deep drink of coffee backed by my Coca-Cola.

"Morning, John." Captain Dick Peters appears tall and commanding (not as sexy as it sounds) over my desk. "I got a fresh case for you. Take a look at this." He plops a manilla folder onto my desk.

"Morning, Captain, how'd you hit 'em last night?"

"I threw down a 285. I'll be damned if we don't take home the big trophy this year."

"Well done, boss. So, what is all this?"

"Something seemingly random. The victim is a white male, 42 years old. Was found in his truck with his head bashed in by a brick. The brick was sitting on the floor of the truck, covered in blood and bone fragments. CSU is still at the scene. I got a bad feeling about this one, John. I think you better head down there."

"Brick huh? Guess that one didn't get laid last night. I'll head over to the scene."

I jot down the address, close the case folder, and return it to its resting place in my file drawer. I give the captain a nod, throw 'good mornings' around the room, and head toward the car.

When you think of a police captain, you are probably already picturing Captain Peters. He's always tan, thin and bald, has a thick Tom Selleck mustache, and his breath always smells a little like coffee and a little like bourbon. Not only is he the

captain of our precinct, he's also the captain of
the GRPD bowling team. They call themselves "Rapid
Fire" and have never taken home the trophy. When
not on duty, the captain dons Hawaiian shirts and
cargo shorts and fills the atmosphere with cigar
smoke and dry dad-jokes. All this being said, when
the captain gets a feeling in his gut, the case
usually turns tough. You'd be a fool not to take the
captain seriously in these situations — probably
why he's the captain — probably why they keep him
as captain.

The Scene

I arrive at the parking lot of 315 Starlite Lane at 8:15 am. The air around the place smells like fried food and grease bins and stale beer. On the property sits Rinaldi's Sports Bar and Grille. Rinaldi's regularly hosts late-night pay-per-view fights that take place not only on the bar's massive pull-down theater screen (and some forty other smaller screens) but sometimes also in the parking lot after any random patron says something along the lines of, "Let's take this outside" or "My dad can take your dad" or "My dick is bigger than yours." The ringside testosterone-driven, sexually repressed energy must get picked up by all those ringside cameras and fed through the broadcast towers and into the twitchy nerves of those heavy-drinking viewers that can lead to any typical night's outcome. Last night though? Well, the captain had a feeling in his gut — didn't he?

"How's it going, John?" CSU's Officer Annie Wilde stands next to the victim's pickup truck.

"Brought you a coffee, Annie."

"Thanks, John. I hope you remembered to add an extra shot."

"A shot of what? As far as I know, they don't have Jameson behind the counter at The Black Hole."

"It's okay, John, I brought my own. So, our victim appears to have had his head bashed in with a brick. The murder weapon is right there." Annie points with a pen toward the floor of the vehicle. There is a pool of blood in the footwell and bits of bone and brain on the murder weapon.

"Your investigative skills never cease to amaze me, Annie," I say with an arguably Clint Eastwood looking smirk.

"I don't think I brought enough Jameson to tolerate you right now Detective Rainey."

Annie looks over a document on a clipboard while I look her over.

"It looks like our deceased, name of Richard Moleski, died from blunt force trauma after being hit several times in the face and head, impacting his skull. We'll call the impacted skull the cause of death for now, John."

"Your investigative ski— "

"—John, I estimate the time of death to be 2:30

AM, June 23, 2019. John, the victim's ID has him at 47 years old and our records indicate he lives in the city of Coopersville with his wife of 30 years, Ellen Moleski. They have 2 children, also in Coopersville. One son, Jeff Moleski; 33, married, also with 2 children, and one daughter and Cassie Moleski; 29, living with the parents."

"So, our friend Richard here picked a fight in the bar with the wrong guy?"

"We don't think so. The position of the victim, combined with the brutality of the attack, suggests a connection between the victim and the potential suspect. It appears as though the victim didn't expect his attacker. I don't think this was your average bar fight, John. Also, the victim has a registered .38 in the glove box; his C&C is in order but as you can see, the firearm didn't do him any good,"

"They rarely do. Well, we know what we know. I'm going to take some pics of the scene and I'll get out of your hair. Tomorrow too soon for a full report?"

"We should have something together by then."

"Okay, I'll drop by tomorrow for the results. Text me if you find anything you might consider a lead."

"Will do, John."

"Thanks, Annie."

Usually, when Annie thinks something seems bigger than it looks, she's right. That being said, I don't have a hell of a lot to go on right now. So, I take my pictures of the victim's truck and anything else that might give me a lead. His truck is Coopersville standard fare. 15-year-old rust-bucket with pro-life decals, a decal of the state of Michigan holding an automatic weapon, and a variety of decals that mention boobs, beer, and of course, another term.

"Tacos, Annie?"

"Question, John?"

"You want to grab a lunch when you're wrapped up here?"

"Does the restaurant have a liquor license?"

"Wherever you want to go."

"Sounds like a plan. I'll text you when I'm about to wrap up."

I toss her a salute and head back to the Goat. Something is pawing at me — doesn't want me to leave the scene. I can't seem to place it. If I did miss

something, Annie would catch it. She's damn good at
her job and not bad on the eyes.

Fill Her Up, Johnny

Blocks from the scene, the Goat and I are heading down Fulton Street and she's thirsty. I pull into the gas station where one of the place's regulars, Jimmy, is standing next to the building with Johnny, the station's attendant. Jimmy is a weathered old black man — his beard and sunglasses barely allow you to make out a face. He wears a large ball cap, sagging from age, and a worn-out Vietnam-era field jacket. He's always wearing that jacket, even in this heat. As I pull up to a pump, Jimmy glances at me without lifting his head. He mutters something to Johnny, eyes looking at me over the top of his glasses. He gets into his old Cadillac to leave. He's acting so nervous that he can barely get his key into the door. I often wonder what I'd dig up if I looked into Jim's background. Probably nothing there at all. Odd that he's never once stuck around when he sees me pull in. Part of me thinks that he just likes to look like he'd done something that would deserve the attention of the law. The guy's a cartoon, a relic from the seventies.

"How's it going, Johnny?"

"Pretty good here, Detective. What's happening

in cop land?"

"Nothing that I can talk about right now, Johnny," I say with that same Clint Eastwood smirk.

Johnny's wearing his station attendant smock over a Clash t-shirt. His fingernails are painted black, and he sports your typical swallow tattoo on the back of his hand. "Anything come down the pipe on my string of missing persons yet?"

"Sorry, boss. If I catch wind of anything, you know I'll hit you up."

We're talking about the same missing persons cases that made a short appearance on my desk this morning. Several missing men who have zero connection to each other have disappeared over the course of several months. There are no leads, no suspects, and no real reason for them to have gone missing. I love the hunt — love the challenge, but this one has me stumped. Johnny here has been slinging smokes and gasoline to every schmo on the West Side. People talk, they always talk, and Johnny here is downwind of all the gossip. You wouldn't call him a snitch. He's just a guy who hears things and pushes those things further downwind. Not to mention, impeccable customer service for such a shithole, west-side, gas station.

"I know you will, Johnny. Enjoy the rest of your

day, man."

"Have a good one, Boss."

"'Detective.'"

The Goat is gassed up, hunched over, and ready to pounce. The smell of gasoline makes her anxious, and it has me wanting to be underneath her. This is as sexy as it sounds. Maintaining Aurelia, and taking care of her, is one of my true off-duty pleasures. Her smell, the fluids, the way she moans when I get her tuned up just right — she does have her stubborn moments; don't we all? If she'd ever been angry with me, it's due to a lack of attention; she usually receives plenty of attention. Sometimes, the job and the winter months keep me away. For now, she's well-fed but the heat has her a little irritated, not unlike the rest of us. At least she's not cooped up in her stall. "We make a good team, old girl."

Outside of the police station, across the street in the park, a small group of protesters have gathered.

Calm, Cool and Collected

January 2017, a man sits at a small workbench in his basement precisely painting a miniature figurine. He is applying a coat of brown to Mrs. Park's overcoat. This man, we'll call him Johnson, has lived a solitary life, enjoyed his home, his hobbies, his neighbors. None of the neighbors know why Johnson never married or if he was married or had any children. They all are curious about Mr. Johnson. They are all curious about everything.

Johnson spent earlier years on the floor of a plant assembling pieces and parts for cars like those so frequently stolen. He'd spent five years waking up, eating breakfast, heading to the plant, assembling, eating lunch, assembling some more, and home. Not long after life at the plant, he did a 5-year stint at Jackson. In the "why" section of the felony question on job applications, he is forced to write the words, "domestic terrorism."

Now applying some black paint to Mrs. Park's headwear, a small television that was perched on an old metal file cabinet showed the inauguration of a new president. "Sheet," he mumbled out loud while switching off the television. He walked slowly, as if far older than he is, up the small wooden staircase and into the kitchen. He took his keys from the wall and headed to his car. The small concrete garage that houses his car has been in a state of repair, by Johnson, for the last 6 years. He gets into his 2000 Buick LeSabre and heads to Ralph's Market for groceries.

A Second Murder

It's dark out. The natives are restless and wild in the streets. Better to be a lion in the jungle than a lion in a swamp. I look beyond the horizon — somewhere out there is an event horizon. A place where crime flips itself on its head and becomes a polar opposite of the city. Somewhere out there is a state sheriff, sitting in a patrol car, waiting for their prey to take the bait. The wide expanse of jurisdiction is haunting me. The drugs are abundant and assuredly homemade. I look at my case files. I wonder if these murders are an act of migration. The deer making their way into the city for lack of food. Perhaps I've been a little closed-minded and have become too comfortable within the shot radius of my blind. It's not often that I question my instincts — my gut usually steers me right. The night calls — I'm letting it go to voicemail.

I wake up to that "Brap-Brap-Brap" and head to the kitchen to begin my routine. That dream has me questioning myself a little, but I'm not falling for it. Regardless, there is something else going on here and I think that it lies outside the bounds of the city. My subconscious has steered me wrong

before, but my gut never has. The event horizon —
a part of the dream. Part of me wants to shut off
the dreams and a part of me doesn't. Unfortunately,
for me, these dreams are the only things in my life
that don't follow a pattern or run on a system —
maybe they are a part of a pattern or a system.
Either way, if I could control them, I would.

I grab my gifted coke and feed this cat. Aurelia
sits patiently, waiting for her ride. I wonder what
Aurelia's dreams would reveal if she had them.

The phone startles me when it starts ringing
wildly — it's Peters.

"Captain?"

"Rainey, we've got another one."

"That's pretty vague, Captain. Another what?"

"Another brick murder."

"Already?"

"Already. This one is at the Comstock Park
Brewery. Get down there asap."

I hang up the phone and start the car; she
growls. I guess that the job does a pretty good
job of putting curves in my road. That being said,
it's my job to straighten them out. I spin the big
round knob on the old push button radio. *Green River*

kicks out of the single speaker inside the front dash and the two speakers at the rear. The sound of the original speaker system is undeniably vintage. This is as much a part of the audible pleasure as the songs that are vibrating through them.

Heading out and regardless the urgency, coffee is a necessary fuel. Like Aurelia, I need my fuel to move, and coffee is my fuel. I stop up to The Black Hole and grab a coffee for me and a coffee for Annie. The job would have had her at the scene through the entire night. I think of her there with her team and all that yellow tape — all those little numbered cards they scatter around marking each specific piece of potential evidence. I wish she would have called me. I'm going to have to suggest that next time she call me.

Arriving at the scene, the Comstock Park Brewery sits near an open field and an old and retired golf course. The brewery is more or less pole barn disguised as a restaurant. You can smell the hops for a 300-yard radius as it wafts through the fields of corn and fields of car parts and seemingly randomly placed old and rusting cars. The brewery also sits on an event horizon, the border between the urban and the rural — this has me questioning my gut, my dream — again.

"Coffee, Annie?"

"You're a lifesaver, John."

"What can you tell me?"

"It's going to be another hot one today."

"You can do better than that."

"Yeah, sorry, I haven't had my coffee yet."

"Well?"

"Another body, John."

"You're the LeBron James of CSU."

"Anyway, John, we have a similar M.O. to last night's murder — another brick, same maker's mark. This victim didn't make it to his vehicle. His vehicle, the van over there, is a 2015 Dodge Caravan with no plates."

"I wonder how anyone could enjoy this hops smell — kind of like hazelnut, how the hell can anyone enjoy hazelnut? Every once in a while, I'll get a coffee from Beaner's, and it has that hazelnut flavor to it. I mean, I won't go to Beaner's anymore. You ever go to Beaner's Annie?"

"His name is Jake Bradly, a 52-year-old male from just up the street. He has a wife and three children, all of them (wife too) are out of the house. Jake also has a record — assault and battery charges, three separate incidents. The latest was

10 years ago."

"I'll get the report."

"The perp appears to have approached our victim from behind, hit him in the back of the head with our brick, then hit him several more times."

"This killer has a chip on his shoulder."

"Looks that way."

"Anything new on our last victim?"

"We are running some tests on the brick. We think we can narrow down where it came from, etc., might get you headed in a direction."

"Dinner tonight?"

"In your dreams, John."

"'Detective.'"

Again, I take in the scene. The van, albeit more of a piece of shit, is dandied up with a similar theme as the last victim's vehicle. The odd ball out is the large decal of a pair of thongs. I'm guessing that the last time this guy saw a pair of thongs was 20-plus years ago. Speaking of playing with others, the stars and bars insignia doesn't exactly play well with others either.

"Hey, Annie, any gun on this one?"

"No gun, John."

"'Detective!'"

"Can't hear ya, John!"

The Apple Don't Fall Far

Dennis, Donnie, Danny, and Tig are standing around a massive bonfire made up of old pallets and chairs and things you find lying around your yard. You can hear side-by-sides, dirt bikes, and four-wheelers running wild through the woods. Not far from the bonfire, there are a couple of bench seats that once served as car seats. There are a couple of old aluminum beach chairs and a fridge, running on an extension cord, plugged in a good fifty yards from its outlet.

"Hey Tig, grab me another beer," Danny yells.

"Get it your damn self, Danny."

"What the fuck did you say?"

"I said, get it your mother-fucking—god—damn—self."

Like a cat from the litter box, Danny springs at Tig and both go to the ground. Danny's got Tig by his neck while Tig squirms and attempts to land a blow on Danny's face. The dust and dirt and bits of leaves swirl and land in their faces and eyes. Dennis, standing about 30 feet from the pair, draws

a Colt out of his drawers and fires off a couple of
shots into the air while simultaneously taking a
drink of his beer.

"God dammit, knock it the fuck off!" He yells
with a distinctive Michigan southern drawl.

The boys stand up, covered in brush and dirt,
and look at Dennis. Tig taps Danny on the arm and
points in Dennis's direction. They both tear after
him like wild fucking banshees. They bring Dennis
and his firearm to the ground.

Donnie doesn't react to any of it — he's higher'n
fuck and a little shit-faced and would rather drink
his beer and watch the embers of the fire crackle
and spit-up little bits of rage.

An old pickup truck rips up to the boys who are
still wrestling on the ground. Another shot, albeit
the sound of a shotgun, rings out across the field.

"You goddamn boys better knock it the fuck off
for somebody gets hurt."

Dennis' Dad, Dave — Dave Green — steps out of the
truck while the boys stand up and brush themselves
off. "I told you sons-a-bitches to stop horsin'
around while you possess a loaded firearm. Did I not
tell you this? Next thing you know, you'll shoot
each other's dicks off, and the goddamn liberals

will have more goddamn ammunition for the war ginst our freedom — you get me?" Dave walks over to Dennis and smacks him upside the head. Some leaves and dirt splish into the air on contact.

Havoc

It's dark out again. I can feel the night penetrating my aura — dominating my nerves. The AC creates the illusion of a chill in the air. I know this illusion will only blind us to the reality that the heat causes violence — causes a rise in the instinct to attack. For this reason, I need to be in it. I need to allow myself to feel what Joe Public feels. Times are tense. Times are more tense than they've been since the towers fell — maybe more so. It's a strange, sweaty, claustrophobic kind of tense. The kind of tension that will turn a neighbor against a neighbor, a partner against a partner, a dog against its owner. Somebody needs to be in it. Somebody needs to patrol it and prevent — it.

The Goat looks ready as she sits alone in the angled ramp of level 4. I admire her beauty. There is a glisten to the car and her surroundings. The humidity creates a mist, a fog, a coating of sweat on everything.

Footsteps resonate through the garage, the kind of footsteps made by a pair of high heels, and bounce of the walls and columns of the ramp. A woman appears. Her milk skin appears unaffected by the humidity, her blue eyes piercing. "Annie?" I say. But it's not Annie.

I'm tempted to turn and head back into the building — this kind of woman usually only appears when she needs someone to take care of a neighbor who lets their yard become unruly or needs a long run of parking tickets taken care of — but instead, I approach her, now standing next to Aurelia.

"Mr. Rainey?" she asks, her voice is soft.

"It's 'Detective' Rainey. How can I be of service."

"You have a choice to make, Detective."

She holds out both of her hands revealing two pills, one red, one blue."

"Are you really standing here trying to sell pills to a cop, lady?"

She places the pills in my hand and wraps my fingers over the pills with both of her hands, all while looking me in the eyes. Everything about this moment is erotic — made more so by her looking me in the eyes.

"Detective, you're going to have to choose one; red or blue, which will it be?"

"This is a tough pill to swallow, lady."

She turns to leave, her heel-to-toe steps continue to echo around the chambers of the parking garage. I look down at the pills when the click clacks of her shoes change pattern. I look toward her to find that the pattern of steps now belongs to a pair of black combat boots on the feet of a sleek black woman. She's wearing an army field jacket and slacks, her hair in cornrows. As she walks away, she lights a cigarette. She tosses a brick onto the floor of the parking ramp and disappears behind a column. For this, I light a cigarette and stand over the brick.

A Break

Aurelia is hungry again — she's always hungry. I pull into the gas station and head toward its small building. Entering, Jimmy mumbles, "ah har hum phrum," followed by, "I gotta gooo, see-yah lay-tah." Jimmy shuffles by Rainey mumbling, "Detective," with a nod and zero eye contact.

"What's his deal?" I ask Johnny. I look toward Fernando, another regular, who is a short, stout Mexican with nothing on his mind but female bosoms that enter and leave the station.

"He gets jumpy around policia," Fernando says. "He says he no trust them. He says is cuz where he grew up."

I look at Fernando and over to Johnny.

"Detective, we might have something for you," Johnny says.

"Yeah? Spill."

"We saw the news, about the guy and the brick."

"Yep." I was annoyed that the media decided to run the story.

"My neighbor," Fernando says, "he has this pile of bricks in his yard, some of them go missing last couple days. Look just like the ones on the TV."

"You don't say?"

"Si. He's a weird dude — keeps to himself. Those bricks have been there forever. Now, some of them are gone. I know because I always wonder why he has those bricks. I kind of want them."

"Don't steal the bricks, Fernando. Thanks for the tip."

"That's what she said," Fernando chuckled while the straw of his fountain drink sat on his lower lip."

I collect the address and throw Johnny a twenty before I head back out to Aurelia.

Time to pay a visit to Annie.

The Boy

March 3rd, 2001, a young man arrives home from a 10-hour day at the factory. His girl sits at a small kitchen table in a small, one-room apartment — her infant child in her arms. The young man hands the young lady a piece of paper — a layoff notice from the GM plant. The young woman starts to cry as she crumples up the paper and throws it at the wall, the child starts crying.

"I got this job, baby, I'll get another one."

"Where, Kam? You know that the Jobs are washing up. We barely scrapin' by as it is." Kam kneels next to her as she puts her hand over her eyes. "We got a child to think of!"

"We got enough to get us by for a month, Nalla. I'll find us somthin'."

"You better do right by us, Kam. Your boy needs you — I need you."

"I'll be looking all-day tomorrow, baby. Let me have a look at our boy."

Nalla's tension isn't penetrating the barrier of positive energy that Kam's own father had instilled in him. During Kam's father's time, jobs were abundant, and it was the only thing Kam knew — regardless of his daddy's goings-on about the seventies and being out of work for months at a time. During Kam's time, there was always food on the table and a roof over his head and a decent car to get around in. The blue-collar black folk neighborhood was full of life as families, all dressed up in matching trousers and fedoras, had summer Sunday afternoon lunches after church — often a neighborhood group activity. Yes, there was little to worry about then — a tussle with a neighbor kid or crushing on little Rosaline were the only concerns for young Kam.

"Don't worry baby, something will come up. I gotch-you."

Pile of Bricks

After my rendezvous with Annie and the deceased, Aurelia and I found ourselves at the house Fernando mentioned at the gas station. It was a long shot, but I had to check the lead. I pulled into the back alley and parked the car. I walked down the alley and, as described, found myself in front of a pile of bricks with the same maker's mark as the bricks used to bludgeon two men to their deaths.

I plug in the address and find that the house is owned by Mr. Kameron Johnson, divorced, 48 years old. I've been to his house before and know this man.

I approach the bricks when a voice, I'm guessing the voice of Mr. Johnson, yells, "What are you doin' there? You just leave them bricks alone."

I raise my hands slightly and take a few steps back. Mr. Johnson appears from his back screen door, gentle in his Malcolm X glasses and a cardigan. I announce myself.

"It's Detective John Rainey. Sir, I'd like to ask you a few questions about these bricks."

"What about my bricks? Somebody been stealin' em. Few gone missin' last few days. Just cuz I ain't got around to usin' em, doesn't make em public domain. Don't see how a couple of missing black man's bricks is GRPD Detective work. I ain't even reported them missing."

"Mr. Johnson—"

"Don't you Mr. Johnson me — I been called Mr. Johnson by enough ya'll in lock-up. Get a warrant or get movin'."

I can see that Mr. Johnson isn't going to budge and doesn't recognize me. I snap a picture of the pile of bricks and head back to Aurelia. Time to make a stop at One Monroe.

Government Mule

"We need a plan. If we don't find a way to regain the public trust, I don't see how we earn another term."

"There's a million ways to beat the system, Micky — a lot of ways. Sometimes, you just need to let the people work it out and sometimes they just need a little push. We'll find what we need — what my people need, Micky. We'll plant some seeds and watch them grow. The soil is ripe for planting, Micky!"

"Yes, Mr. President."

"Let's go get a taco bowl, Micky. I love me a good taco bowl."

Apples

A few days before the first murder, Dennis, Donnie, Danny, and Tig are all piled into Donnie's 1978 Monte Carlo and headed toward the city. Big thumps from a big speaker is feeding the fire that erratically burns, contained only by the steel and glass of the Monte Carlo.

"Man, you can't even see out this back window with this shitty tint job you did."

"Fuck you, Danny. At least my car runs."

Danny plants a fist into Donnie's right shoulder. The Monte swerves into the other lane of this two-lane backroad.

"Jesus Christ you fuckheads, keep your shit together, you gonna get us pulled over," Dennis says while rolling a smoke.

Pantera's *Cowboys from Hell* is blasting out of the speakers. In the trunk, 800 grams of methamphetamine is on its way to a dealer on the northwest side of the city.

"Man, fuck the cops," shouts Donnie.

"Fuck you, man — the cops prolly on our side anyway," Danny replies.

"Fuck you guys, I ain't going to jail." Tig was always twitchy, his blonde rat tail made him look extra twitchy.

"Aight, cool it, fuckers," says Dennis. Let's get this drop moved and get the fuck back home." The three roll into the driveway of their distributor.

Tommy Polaski - The Polish Dog, is standing inside the screen door of his house. He's bare fucking naked and his face looks like a pumpkin that sat out for an entire winter. Donnie pops the trunk open and removes a large camo duffle bag. The four head up to the porch.

"What the fuck happened to you, man?" Tig shouts up to Tommy as they climb up the porch steps.

"Some fucking bitches from last night — don't fucking worry about it," Tommy replies while opening and holding the screen door open.

As the boys walk in, a naked girl, who looks about 17, is sprawled out on Tommy's couch.

"Daaaamn, maaan," Danny says as he spies the girl. She turns her body a little on the couch and the motion is somehow erotic. This is especially true when it comes to the likes of Dennis, Donnie, Danny, and Tig.

Tommy, responding to Danny's excitement over the girl in his usual calm and relatively stern manner, "That's why they call me the Polish fucking Dog. Let me see this shit." Tommy reaches for the bag.

"Yeah man, this is one of our best batches. You'll clear this shit in no time," Donnie says.

"Yup." Tommy, still naked, grabs an envelope off of the coffee table that is covered in bongs and bowls, pipes and beer cans, and hands it to Dennis. "Get the fuck out of here now." During this sentence, Tommy had become semi-erect. Tig is standing near the entryway trying not to laugh at the erection.

"Cool." Dennis stands up and the boys follow suit. Tommy extends his hand to shake. Dennis, reluctantly, reaches out and shakes Tommy's hand.

As the boys head down the steps, Tig can't help himself and busts out laughing. "Good thing you shook his hand and not his dick," Danny says as the boys try not to laugh too hard and loud.

"I think you made him hard," Danny says to Dennis.

"I still got it! All bitches, male and female gotta get off on this shit."

Tig shouts from the back seat, "Fuck man, that's fucking sick!"

The four boys rip out of the driveway and fling the Monte around the corner. They damn near scrape a cop car who immediately put on his lights. The boys decide to play cool and keep driving. After the cop makes his U-turn, shots are fired from somewhere in the vicinity, and he redirects the car toward the shots. The boys take off down quiet roads and back alleyways to evade any further interactions with the cops.

As the boys pass Fulton Street, Larry and Paul are standing on the corner waiting to cross. They wave at the boys in the Monte Carlo as it passes. The boys, as boys do, give the two men the finger.

"Jeez, Larry — what did we ever do to them?"

"You got meeee!" says Larry while waving around an imaginary 2x4. "Bet their moms wouldn't be too happy about that!"

"No, Larry, I don't think so either."

The little walking man signals green, and Larry and Paul make their way across the street. They pass Ray, a 7-foot-tall man, wearing the same red sweatshirt he wears every day, over the same button-down white shirt that he wears every other day, who never stops twirling the cowlick on the top of his head. Ray is headed back from the gas station with his daily 2-litre of Mountain Dew. Larry and Paul are headed to the gas station for their 2-litres of coke that they will bring down to the river and enjoy while catching catfish. All of these men are not dressed for the heat. Doesn't seem to bother any of them.

One Monroe

That brick pile sits in a pocket of my gut. Not sure if I should give the media credit for this one. Hopefully, this doesn't lead me on a wild goose chase — A wild goose chase, where the hell did that phrase come from?

"What do you have, Rainey?"

"Captain, I have a lead, a small one, regarding these serial jobs. We have a pile of bricks at the house of one Mr. Kameron Johnson. Do you remember him? He wasn't keen on me poking around his house."

"You want a warrant?"

"I feel like it's worth looking into."

"You think it's going to set off any red flags?"

"I don't think so. I'd like to get some tests done on the bricks to rule them, and Mr. Johnson, out."

"Okay, talk to the Judge."

After spending some time getting the affidavit off, I decide to drop over to CSU and see if Annie's around. Nothing like dropping into forensics to give you a kick in the ass and make you feel a little stupid. I trail my way through the CSU office and into the garage. Annie is hunched over a car, wielding a camera.

"What's going on Officer Annie Wilde?" I'm such a putz.

"Detective John Rainey, what did I do to deserve your rays of sunshine?"

"Thought I would pull a surprise house-call and make sure that no laws were being broken."

"Good one, John. Did you spend all night coming up with that one?"

"Thought that one up when I decided to become police. I've said that line more times than I can count."

"That's great, John. So, bricks are the same bricks used to pave Wealthy Street. Metropolitan Brick Company. We think they were purchased from a local supplier, the same supplier who sold them to the city — R.J. Robinson Masonry. R.J. Robinson specializes in antique or restored brick as well as new. Not sure if that gets you any leads. If you find a suspect with a cache of bricks, we can use our magic powers to match them up — to an extent."

"Well, as soon as I get the warrant for Mr. Kameron's bricks, we'll have something to run those tests on."

"You think you have a solid lead?"

"Sigh, I'm not sure just yet. Right now, I'm just following up on a lead that ran upstream. In my gut, this isn't our guy. It's too easy, too obvious. That and Kameron isn't a smash a guy in the head with a brick sort of guy."

"You know a lot of smash a guy in the head with a brick kinda guys?"

"No, but I've had a few exes that might demand that reputation."

"Fair enough. You probably instigated it though. There are times—"

"There are times you want to smash me in the head with a brick?"

"I plead the fifth."

"No contest."

"Jesus."

"You hungry?"

"Always."

"Let's go."

"With you?"

"…"

"…"

"Let's go."

Brick Oven

"Annie and John walk into a bar… or a brick oven pizzeria that just so happens to have a bar." This place is full of that old-world, modern charm. One wonders if the baby grand in the corner still has its guts or is more of a prop like the Marshall Stack amplifiers that line the back wall of any concert from the 80s.

"Seat yourself," a sign directs us as we walk through the door.

"Bossy Place," Annie says while pointing at the sign.

"If the sign wasn't there, people would be standing in line from last week."

"You have so little faith in people, John."

"Hey now, I had faith that the gentleman who greeted us at the door would ask for some change."

"Some things are obvious, John."

"So are some Judges."

"Good choice on the giant brick oven restaurant

on a ninety-degree day, John."

"In the winter, you'll wish you were here again."

"I wish it was snowing in here right now."

"I'm sure you do, Annie. Nobody knows cold like you."

"Ice cold, John… Ice cold."

"How's the love life, Annie?"

A waiter interrupts our fascinating banter. "Hey guys, what can I start you off with?" She is young. She almost looks too young to be serving. Apparently, I've reached the age where adults look like kids, and I look like an old man.

Annie orders her usual. "I'll have a whiskey, neat."

I order a Coke.

"John, I'm going to keep an eye on you. I know how you get when you've had too many Cokes."

"At this point, I'm pretty sure that your whiskey has little to no effect on you, regardless the quantity."

"Ahh to be intolerant to alcohol again, one can dream, John… one can dream."

"What do you want on your pizza?"

"Everything, John."

"Everything?"

"Everything."

"Jesus."

"Live a little John."

"You know, every time we hang out you tell me to live a little, do you think that by telling me to live a little that some magic door will open for me? Do you think that by throwing caution to the wind, I'll find something new to occupy my time? Do you think that if I get completely shit-faced that you'll have a chance with me? Let me tell you something honey, It'll take a lot more than a copy of Detroit Living to get me in the sack."

"Oh common, John. If I threw you a five-dollar bill, you'd have to arrest yourself for prostitution."

"Do you have a five?"

"I most certainly do not."

"I hear that the bartender from Maggie's will put out for a twenty."

"You hear?"

"I can't recall the last time I had a twenty."

"All that overtime and nothing to show for it?"

"I have a very good record collection to show for it."

"You can't take it with you."

"I'll try."

"You wanna go fool around, John?"

"Probably not a bad idea. It'd be good for morale."

"In the name of camaraderie!"

"For the force… for the good guys!"

"For the good gals!"

"Let's get out of here."

I wasn't known to "fool around" but now and again find the act of "fooling around" to be a good way to clear the mind and relieve some stress. The banter between Annie and I serves as a kind of foreplay and continues into our fooling around. One thing I am also certain about is that most of the force doubts our heterosexuality. I don't blame them; I often doubt Annie's heterosexuality and I'm certain that she also questions mine. It stems more from our lack of desire to throw our sexuality around.

When we are working, which is most of the time, that's all we are doing. Well, that and bantering each other into our own sexual submissions.

After an intense, sweaty, and passionate romp, Annie always lights up a smoke. There are very few times in a week when I might enjoy a cigarette but sharing a cigarette with Annie after sex is one of life's small greatest pleasures. For some reason, this is also when I choose to let Gilbert into the house to enjoy a saucer of coffee creamer. This is probably the closest I'll ever get to the all-American family. It's all I can afford or that can afford me. The work will always come first, I resolved to this fact many years ago after Veronica broke off our engagement. As he stormed out of our apartment, my favorite Coltrane record amongst the things she would carry out, she yelled that I'd end up Lennie Briscoe, destined to routinely make jokes about my many ex-wives. Far be it me to disappoint. Nevertheless, I decided, at that moment, that I would just be a cop and not be a Lennie Briscoe kinda cop — with a trail of broken ex-wives. If I wanted kids, they would have ended up in the full custody of these ex-wives. Hell, I'm surprised they haven't taken old Gilbert away from the residence — it's not like the county has ever been very good regarding animal control and regulation. It is the Sheriff's department after all. Far be it me to criticize the organization that routinely lets prisoners escape.

"Now that you've fed your pussy," Annie motions in Gilbert's direction, "you wanna go another round?"

"Frankly, Annie, I don't give a damn."

"In that case, I'll just have my way with you."

"Far be it me to argue with a CSU officer."

"I brought handcuffs, John."

"It's 'Detective,' did you bring the key for those cuffs?"

"Nope."

"Shit."

A Request of Utmost Importance

"Micky?"

"Sir?"

"Micky, I need to make a statement to my social media followers."

"Okay, sir. What would you like to say today?"

"I'm not sure. What day is it today, Micky?"

"It's the Fourth of July, sir."

"Great, that's just great. The Fourth of July, Micky, what a great day to be a patriot."

"Did you want to post something about the Fourth of July, Sir?"

"Of course I do, Micky, I should say something about freedom, don't you think so, Micky?"

"I'd say that freedom is a safe bet, Sir."

"How about something like, 'The Fourth of July is just great.' How does that sound, Micky?"

"I think you might try something with a little more substance, Mr. President."

"Substance… Okay Micky, let's say something like, 'The Fourth of July is really, super great. Americans, ask the media how great this day is. You know what? The media will never understand how great this day is and should be ashamed of themselves for all their fake news. Together, we can make this country greater.' What do you think of that, Micky?"

"I think we can revise it a little bit, Sir."

"Too late."

"Too late?"

"I posted it with a picture of myself in front of the flag, Micky. People are going to love it! Look at this picture of me in front of the flag, Mick. Don't you love it?"

"Yes, Mr. President. It's a fine picture."

"We should get a Coney Dog, Mickey. What a great day for a Coney. Don't you think a Coney sounds good right now, Micky?"

"Yes sir, a Coney dog sounds fine."

"Sure does, Mick. Let's ask Google or Alexis where to get a good Coney Dog. I'm buying, Mick."

The Fourth of July

It's hot, even for morning. Today is the Fourth of July — and tonight is also the Fourth of July. Amateur hour to the patriots out there. This Fourth, there is a storm brewing originating from the voice of independence, a fierce heatwave that will trigger forest fires and hurricanes and drought.

She walks toward me in the shadows of the parking garage.

I'll be a fierce hunter today. The broken-down system of ill colored blood and black and blue will cover up all of the mindless Parker Posey, rosy-cheeked and lighter-driven mischief. Abandoned simple truths regarding an empire run by flourishing perfume dealers. They couldn't handle the cocaine or the beginning of an idea. Mothers and fathers of both comfort and strife, entitlement and the entitled — *they* will find a way to paint the town with a hyper-color and ill-gotten patriotism. All of this comradery will be summed up in one big fat gulp from Aurelia at pump number two. What used to be a series of turning wheels escalating up-up-up is now a series of digital lines that intersect and shift while retaining the same old spirit of up-up-

up. During an election year the slogans should be as simple as, "vote for an asshole and save a buck," or, "vote for a kinder asshole and spend a buck." At the end of the day, the buck stops in a beat-up old ford with a brick on the floor.

Drinking my coffee on the patio allows me the routine hour of catching up with the news. I still have a traditional newspaper delivered to my house but rarely look at it. I have it delivered because it's the way it's always been and I'm not one for change. I'm not completely removed from scrolling social media or news streams on my iPad. Whatever Clint Eastwood dick you might have dreamed up can't possibly be all there is to a person or a cop. There is a lot to consider in the wild and indefinite scroll. There is a blanket of cute and supernatural beauty that clouds loneliness and sadness and all the things that hurt people from day to day. There is a layer of soapbox yelling and preaching that goes on at a surface level—reactions to whatever sets a fucking person off on any given day. There is another layer, somewhat hidden between the lines within the scroll — a tumultuous mob rage — or union of spirits — intersecting in the heart and in the soul, brewing up a big idea. This being said, any big idea will have its counterpart — an iniquitous plot that will do everything possible to keep the big new idea pushed into a junk drawer alongside the scissors and the tape and the pile of old, dried-up Bic pens and empty Bic lighters.

While I sit here scrolling and sipping my coffee, I'm shocked by the loud and sudden crack of a mini explosive over my head. The excitement around popping off little bits of paper in the air will take over everything for the next two days — one or two fingers will pay the ultimate price. Near my residence is not only the jail, but a street that separates the comfortable elite from the working-class scrapers. Both sides of the street will be a fury of cracks and pops and quick, bright lights that set off the animals' and veterans' PTSD — those who should be celebrated the most on Independence Day. These are the some guys, or some gals, who saw some shit and perhaps killed some people and abandoned their own life to serve. They are those with no reward and ask for none. Proud of the freedom you read about in Grandpa's letters home but struggling to find their place within said freedom.

And so, as I scroll, the internet is talking about the brick murders in all of my streams. The reality of these murders has slipped to the side and taken on some kind of comic book idealism, that is rendered in black and white ink, while leaving so much room for the imagination. One group is violently screaming about the wall at the border allowing treacherous immigrants in to kill our wholesome family unit with fentanyl — the other side has morphed our killer into a vigilante of justice who has been beaten down enough by tireless Nazi scum. Both sides are lit fuses on dynamite — dynamite with sprinkles of lavender set in amongst the gunpowder. If social media asked me, the police sketch tells me this is a broken man who was set off by something singular. His reaction is not to kill. Maybe, just maybe, this isn't freedom's ring. These bricks don't pop or crack. There isn't really any wow factor in the sound of a thud.

An event reminder pops up on my screen. There is a backyard barbeque tonight at the captain's house. "Hawaiian attire is preferred," it says in the invite. Okay, Peters — It just so happens that I have the same Hawaiian shirt that Elliot Gould wore in the movie version of M*A*S*H. Only me, and possibly Annie, will understand both the sentiment and statement in wearing this shirt. Nobody needs to know that I have both a sense of humor and a passionate dislike for politicking. I'm just a cop after all — what the fuck do I know about politicking?

Gilbert the cat surprises me with his butt in my face. He's rubbing the side of his face on my iPad and checking the contents of my coffee cup.

"How'd you get back here mister?"

The cat doesn't respond.

"Care for a donut, officer?"

Neighbor Victoria appears with a box of Van's donuts, wearing a light robe and a pair of Ugg slippers. She has a can of Diet Coke in her other hand. Case closed on the Coke while the doughnuts suggest a similar comedic symbolism to that of my Trapper John shirt.

"Hey, Vic, what brings you and the cat into my backyard?"

"John, we hardly know each other but have been neighbors for so many years. I thought it'd be nice to spend some time getting to know one another. Don't you think?"

I've never been sure if she was flirting or prying. I suppose that now is as good a time as any to find out.

"You've brought doughnuts, you sure do know the way to a cop's heart. Have a seat here, would you like a cup of coffee?"

"Do you have any tea, John?"

"I do… I'll be right back."

I haven't made a cup of tea in a stint. Through the kitchen window, it'd be hard for one not to admire her looks while she's out there at the table petting Gilbert. She has long brown hair and big brown eyes and features that might qualify a woman's woman. She's tall with curves and at the same time lean. Her hands are a woman's hands, and her fingernails and toenails are a vivid red. My hands, on the other hand, are soft but filled with the residue of gunpowder.

What if she's the brick killer? I think to myself as the water comes to a boil. Wouldn't that be a twist? I believe anything's possible these days. Stranger than fiction they say — the fiction these days is less strange anyway. The writings and their readers are as idealistic as the influencers' perfect made-up worlds of peace and love while their tongues hang out and they stand in front of some bullshit waterfall. Edit out all the tourists with sweat-filled shirts and cameras and kids. Nothing to hate about it, nothing to love about it. Just cutesy and safe sugar cookies with an old-fashioned on the side to add some sense of strange.

"Here you go, Vic," I note that her robe has somehow found itself a way to reveal more of her chest — maybe the robe is flirting with me.

"So, John, what made you become a police officer?"

She asks as though there was ever some sort of watershed moment that put me here.

"I'm a detective. I'm here because I need to be here. Without law, there is no order, Vic."

"Really?" The roll in her eyes let me know that she is smarter than to fall for that.

"Haha no — not really, maybe a little? My dad was police, and my grandfather was police. It's just the way it goes. You're brought up around this job and bleed it. The practice is as common as a ten-dollar trinket in the dollar store."

"I get that, I'm not like that though. My mom was a wife and mother, as was her mother; came before anything else. It wasn't until the divorce that she had to become independent. From the split, we also became friends."

"What did she do?"

"She opened a retail store and did pretty well with it. Now we run a small franchise of stores together. Did you ever rebel against your police family, John?"

"That's a tough one for me, Vic. Let's save that level of introspection until we know each other a little better. So — you're the one that's been leaving the Coke outside my door?"

"Guilty. You gonna arrest me?"

"Maybe."

"There are a lot of fun responses that I could slip in here, John."

"I can think of a few. So, Vic, what do you have planned for the fourth?"

"Heading out to Saugatuck for the weekend — mom's place near the beach is an annual tradition — pretty standard fare. How about you?"

"Cop barbecue at captain's house, also pretty standard fare."

"Speaking of, I should probably get my ass moving. We'll have to do this again, John."

"Let's try not to make a habit of it."

"So we'll settle for small holidays and an occasional weekend?"

"Sounds fair…"

"I'll have my lawyer draft something up."

"I'll sign it as soon as it hits my desk."

Vic opened the gate — it would be hard not to

admire her grace in that robe as she moved. Her ankles floated above her small feet and could easily sell tickets. The cat went with her. I was tempted to go with her.

I gather my iPad and my newspaper and my coffee cup and her coffee cup and head in for a shower. I'm hoping that Annie will be at this thing. I shoot her a text, bare fucking naked, before hopping in the shower.

Jesse

I'm out the door with a bottle of wine and wearing my Trapper John Hawaiian print shirt over some dockers. Peters lives on the West Side off of Leonard. During the drive, most of the streets are empty save for the little gatherings outside of each of the shit-hole bars. Annie did text me back and asked if I could pick her up and I don't see why I wouldn't. Showing up together gives everyone something to talk about during downtime, as if downtime was ever a thing. I suppose it's also something to chatter about at the cop bar.

Out of the corner of my eye, I catch the erratic motions of a pushing match in the parking lot of shit-hole number three. Jesse, an old run-in, is going at it with some kid. I've gotten to know Jesse a little over the years. We've had some occasional red flags, and he lives on my old beat. The kid he's about to get into it with looks like your average scrapper. Camo cargo shorts, and a tank top and flip-flops, make nice combo on a one-hundred-pound, soaking-wet kid. The fourth has always brought out Jesse's best. PTSD and Jim Beam make him hard to handle on holidays. Just as Jesse is pulling back to

clock this guy, I pull in and yell his name through
Aurelia's window. Both opponents are startled by my
yapping while three other kids run out of the bar
to collect their nearly floored companion. I get out
of the car and head over.

"Jesse."

"Rainey."

"You know it's not in your best interest to be
hanging around this place so early in the day. There
are a lot of hours left and only trouble coming down
that bottle." Jesse lights a cigarette and squints.
I take off my Ray Bans and ask him for one. He taps
his pack of cigarettes against his hand releasing a
single cigarette and offers it to me. I take it and
light it. "Head on home, Jess," I tell him. "Put on
a movie and take it easy and tune out all the shit
in your head. You hearing me?"

"Yeah — Okay, Rainey."

A tan Monte Carlo goes barreling out of the
parking lot. A screech and some yelling and several
sets of middle fingers is all directed at me and
Jesse. Jesse drops his cigarette on the ground,
stifles it with his boot, and puts on his sunglasses.
His leather skin, stubble-covered and weathered,
nods in my direction before moving toward the
direction of an old pickup truck.

"You good to drive, Jesse?"

"I'm good."

"Good enough for me."

Time to pick up Annie.

Barnstorming

"Let's go back and get that motherfucker!" Danny gripes from the back seat of the Monte Carlo.

Donny, driving and pissed off spouts back, "Settle the fuck down, Danny. That guy was going to knock your fucking lights out and you know it. If that asshole in the GTO didn't show up, you be in the fucking hospital. Ask me, you had it coming the way you were running your mouth in the bar. Mother fucker served in Afghanistan and had to listen to you running your mouth about fucking sand-niggers. I half want to stop the fucking car and beat your ass right here! You better hope the old man doesn't catch wind of your bullshit, Danny."

"Let's just take a deep fucking breath and calm the fuck down," says Dennis to the group. Tig is in the back next to Danny and nods along to Dennis' plea. "Ya'll know we aren't going to say anything to the old man. We all had some shots, and we all got a little overstimulated and we all need to fuck-ing simmer-the-fuck down. We're going to go home and build a big fucking bonfire and rip around the field and shoot some guns. Uncle Dan is bringing a fresh keg, and we have plenty of fucking fireworks to light off all night. Donny, put on some fucking music."

Donny clicks on the head unit and *Walk* starts blaring through the car speakers. Dennis reaches over and ejects the CD. "Let's find something a little less fucking angsty, god dammit." He pulls the cd binder from the floor and grabs Ludacris, sliding into the deck. "Fucking better."

The crew rolls back to Allegan while rapping along to Ludacris and smoking a fat joint. The goddamn car looks like it's interior is on fire.

Pig Roast

"Jesus Christ Peters, I didn't think you'd be roasting a pig!"

"You only get one go-around, right John? Hey Annie, do you want to do a quick autopsy on the pig? The victim's hot."

"Fucking, Peters."

"Haha! Good to see you too Annie. Why don't you two grab some beers and mingle a little — I don't want John here to get any ideas around this pig."

"I'm not sure what you just said, Captain. I might need a few beers to understand your pig-Latin."

"Fuck me, John," Annie says. "Remind me how Jerry Seinfeld was able to make it in the laugh game with you alive and spitting out fire like that?"

"Annie, you're the Andrew Dice Clay of crime scene investigators."

"Bada-Boom, John."

"Both of yous clearly need a beer before you should be allowed to talk. Beer's right over there," the captain says while pointing in the direction of a second patio. "Go mingle. Quit being so damn antisocial."

"Annie, I think Dick here just gave us a good tip."

"I'd have to agree, John. Not only do I agree with Dick's tip, but I also agree wit yous."

"After you, my dear."

"I insist."

"I'm earning this Trapper John shirt today."

"You sure are John, if I'd known better, I would have worn a Hot Lips cheerleader outfit."

"I don't think the boys in blue could handle you in that."

"You come around here much?"

"First time."

"Let's take Peter's advice and mingle a little. I'd hate to seem haughty."

"I agree. We don't want the commoners to think haughty of us."

"John! Glad you made it!" Gladstone and Richards seem to appear from nowhere. "Annie, how are you?

Did you both get in your fill of Dick's pig jokes yet?"

"We didn't have time to prepare for this one, Gladstone."

"Yeah, neither did we." Richards chuckles to himself as though he made a joke.

"How you coming on that whole brick case, John?" asks Gladstone.

"Not a lot to go on right now. Some coincidences and a pallet of bricks but no solid leads. How about you guys? Did you get any closer to that dealer?"

"Naw," replies Richards. "Every time we think we got a solid lead, shit goes dark. I don't think this guy's a pro, I think it's just some dumb luck bullshit. We almost got to this clown over on the southwest side who's been moving shit around. He won't talk though, guess he ain't the type."

Several hours pass and several similar conversations weave in and out and around Peters' backyard. Annie and I pull an Irish Goodbye and settle into The Goat.

"You want to grab a coffee?" Annie asks as I settle into Leonard Street.

"I could use it; you think we left too early?"

"I think we didn't leave early enough."

"Let's go have coffee at my place, I don't know if anything is open right now, Annie. It's a fucking holiday."

"Your place, huh? Let's make it my place."

"Why your place, you looking to slip me a mickey?"

"Maybe."

"Then your place it is."

Annie has a pretty typical West Side home. A small brick ranch, built in the 1950s, it has a small yard and a typical one-stall garage. The inside of her place is mostly utilitarian. She doesn't have a television in her living room but does have one in the bedroom. The furniture is sparse but is all Eames or Herman Miller furniture. Her bookshelf's book collection is extensive. On the walls of the living room, she has all of these posters from the Herman Miller company picnics. One time, I asked her about her obsession with the brand. She told me about her grandfather's stories of working at Herman Miller. He was an assemblyman and most of the furniture was stuff she'd inherited from him — the posters too. She mentioned something about the Johnny Cash song, *One Piece at a Time* — said that a lot of the stuff was either defects or parts that her grandpa smuggled out of the factory. She has a strong connection to the brand and her sentiment is pretty cool and undoubtedly in good taste.

"It might be a warzone outside but who would know or care?" I yell to Annie who's in the kitchen. I ask her if she'd like to step outside and check out the show before she emerges from the kitchen in a nightgown.

She asks me if I'd like to check out the show.

And so it goes.

Fifth of July

The parking garage is void of any cars save for Aurelia. I'm propped up in a Herman Miller Eames plywood chair with an interrogation lamp over my head. Some fella in a black suit and black tie is sitting across from me. He has no eyes. He's tapping his fingers on a round wooden table before reaching over and pressing the record button on a small tape recorder.

"Mr. Rainey," he says, "do you mind if I record our conversation?"

I don't respond.

"Mr. Rainey, I think you already know that it is in both of our best interests if you cooperate. Let me repeat the question; Mr. Rainey, do you consent to the recording of our conversation?"

I respond with, "What's this all about."

"Mr. Rainey, I can't talk to you unless you consent. Why do you insist on making this difficult for both of us. Like you, I have a job to do. Don't worry, Mr. Rainey, no harm will come to you or your friend Annie."

"What's Annie got to do with this."

"I'm sorry, Mr. Rainey. What part of my last request did you fail to understand?"

I wake up and look for my clock. I realize that my surroundings are not my own. I reach over to Annie's warm body and go for my phone.

"John, what time is it," Annie quietly asks.

"It's early, Annie. I'm going to head home and get ready for work. I'll call you later."

"Okay, John."

I dress and I kiss her on the forehead and head out.

Suspended in the fog of the morning still lingers the smell of sulfur and charcoal. I trip a little over the remnant of a burnt-up canister and am compelled to remove my firearm and take a shot at it. Aurelia's top and hood have little bits of paper and ash scattered about. I'm compelled to tell her I'll get her clean as I open her heavy door and smell her scent. No "new-car" scent could ever compare to the scent that exudes from Aurelia.

We cut through the fog and mist long before the sun can burn it all off. Friday morning after a holiday. Folks will barely do what's required of them to get back to the spirit of spirits. Before all of the festivities resume, I need to get my shower, my coffee and my run in. Without those things, I'm about as useless as Gilbert hanging around a porch. I park the car and head into the house for that coffee.

Third Time's the Charm

My run is in, and my shower is done and my coffee is brewing when I get the call. A man was beaten to death outside of a sports lounge. A brick was found at the scene. This same night, another missing man was also reported who fits the description of the other missing persons in my missing persons' case. Happy Fifth of July.

So I head out, en route to another scene that would surely reflect a human nature we've all thought about nurturing (at least verbally) ("I'll fucking kill you") on so many occasions. Less an instinct or two to not lose everything or perhaps not burn in hell. There might be a fine line between greed and resurrection. In somebody's bible the brick might be a tool of salvation — an act on a god's behalf, while in another bible — thou shalt not kill with a brick. The color is another thought-provoking theme. The color of these bricks is just enough brown that the soaked-up blood in their crevices and crevasses renders a rich textured brown similar to what you might find on your shoe after a run. Either way, the end result is Goliath or David or the people in those Judean Foothills. Somebody here is going to

hell or in hell — hell, on July 5th in 1776, this was
probably true for the lot of them. After all, some
kid is probably playing a trumpet somewhere in the
world — hell, there probably always is.

I roll up to a scene not unlike but still
different from the others. At this scene, I know
the car. It's Tommy Polaski, a two-bit dime store
hustler's car. Tommy deals all over this town.
He's the one who will get your little girl hooked
on pills and work her up toward the hard stuff.
She's lucky if he doesn't impregnate her while he's
grooming her for an overdose. Not only is this prick
the poster boy for scumbags united, he's also an
old-school skinhead like his daddy and his daddy's
daddy. The poofy flight jacket, suspenders and Fred
Perry bullshit might add up to another punk-rock,
working-class motif. But in this case, Polaski's
hatred for anything off-color starts with the giant
swastika tattoo on his back (and his chest, and
his dick) that bleeds through his skin and into
his heart or brain or whatever organ makes these
assholes tick. If it weren't for the brick that's
sitting next to his dead fucking body, I'd say it
was well past his time. It's not fitting that he
should go down during a serial string; he doesn't
deserve the publicity. If I can, I'll keep the media
as limited in knowledge of this one as possible.
This is the one murder that turns this killer into

some kind of vigilante hero. Right now, times are ripe for mob mentality. People are agitated and bored and hot and ready to go off like so many M80 fireworks on the Fourth of July. This little string of serial murders might just be the prologue to a long story called 2019.

For now, I will spare the back-and-forth dialogue between Annie and Myself. Let's just say that we both end up at a stalemate.

Tommy-fucking-Polaski. Cock-sucker.

The Man

On July 5th, 2016, Kam spent most of the day looking for work while Nalla was working a line in a small dowel factory. Their infant child, Troy — now fifteen, stayed late after school for a band fundraising event.

After arriving home and while standing in their kitchen, Kam and Nalla are arguing about work and money and bills — an argument they've been having for fifteen years.

At 4:45 pm, on the corner of Cass and Jefferson, Troy lay on the sidewalk with his backpack on his back and his trumpet case in his arms, motionless. First responders arrived on the scene exactly 6 minutes after the boy was shot, this was both GRFD and GRPD. An ambulance arrived 3 minutes later but none of them arrived early enough to catch the last breath from the boy. Troy was shot three times, two shots hit him in the arm and side while the third shot hit him in the neck.

Immediately following the shooting, Officer Rainey and his fellow police didn't have a lot of work to put in. The shooter was given up almost immediately — by his mother.

When you have to get in your car and drive to one parent's home to inform them that their child has been murdered by another parent's son, the term work becomes subjective. This family was ruined, and it was at this moment that their foundation had begun to crumble. A building, metaphorical in some respect, would still be erected on this crumpled-up and cracked foundation where these mothers had started their lives. This foundation — the house upon it — would always serve as a heart-breaking and dangerous place to lay your head.

A-Plus

"Mickey, you see this article in my news feed?"

"No, Sir. Your feed is only yours, Sir."

"Ha-ha, very funny. You are a very funny man, Mick. Anyway, did you see this thing that happened in Michigan?"

"If you mean the string of serial murders, then yes, I am aware of the news."

"Crazy… To think that somebody would go around just murdering people with bricks like that. The media will probably find a way to blame me for it, Mick. Like I could, in any way, have anything to do with what's going on all the way in Michigan. The media, let me tell you, Mick. You know, if I had to give a dollar to Ted Koppel every time the media had something nice to say about me, I'd be a very rich man, hey Mick?"

"I'm not sure how that math works out, Sir."

"Mick?"

"I mean — absolutely sir, ha-ha, you'd be the richest man on earth."

"Funny how that works, isn't it? We better nip this thing in the tit, Mick. Get our guys in here and let's talk about a game plan. I'm certain that they'll blame me for this. Fake, fake, fake — liars all of them. I should probably post something about this."

"Sir, I—"

"Mick, go get our team. We need to nip this thing in the pussy."

"I always get the job done. A-plus, Sir… Count on it."

"I know you do, Mick — I know you do."

Skrewdriver

Tommy-fucking-Polaski. I fail to make the connection — I fail to make the connections on any of this. Maybe I'm getting rusty or maybe I'm getting cloudy. Maybe it's from the early-late night romps — this new sweat-inducing break from routine could be muddling up my instincts. There is something that breaks in a man when it comes to passion around women. I'm not above any of the endorphin-releasing masculinity that has been reflected so many times in the movies. If it can happen to Kirk, it can happen to me. Either way, I can't let it get in the way of this work. The job is what I gave up all that Lenny Briscoe stereotype for.

I quickly become obsessed with the thought that I'd missed something crucial at the Polaski crime scene and in the case in general. Some small detail must have been overlooked. So, I'm sitting at my desk staring deeply into each photograph from the crime scene and re-watching and reviewing, over and over again, the footage from each location's cameras. It's all piling up — overwhelmingly so.

"John," the captain belts out from his office, "could you come in here a minute?"

I close up my case files and head to the office. I can see two stereotypical figures through the slatted blinds of the captain's office windows and I already know what this is going to be.

"John, I'd like you to meet Special Agents Mike Mullins and Kate Simms." The captain looks toward the two figures. "Agents, this is Detective John Rainey." Both agents share a nod in my direction, and I return with the same subtle salutation. "John, I was talking with the Chief of Police, along with our mayor, and we thought it would be best to bring in some federal profilers. I know I should have talked to you first but—"

"—I completely agree captain."

"You completely agree, John? Did I hear you right?

John, you're not putting up a fight? I'm considering sending you to our resident nutcracker."

"With all due respect Captain, I'm dealing with a string of missing persons that have no connection, rhyme or reason, or leads, and now these brick murders are also leaving me dry. Sir, I don't know if I'm losing it or what — I know I've been distracted lately and am looking to remedy that. In the meantime, I think I could use the brainpower here. Maybe Agents Mullins, and Simms here, can help put me right."

Agent Mullins chimes in, "We will certainly use our resources to accommodate in any way we can, Mr. Rainey." He adjusts his necktie while saying this line. I bet he rehearsed the necktie routine and acts on it every time he makes this little statement. He probably learned it at Quantico.

"It's 'Detective' Rainey."

"Agents, could you give the detective and me a few minutes?"

"No problem," says Simms.

The two agents leave the room and Peters offers me a chair.

"Take a chair, John."

"Captain, I—"

"John, is everything okay? I mean — I know this is a lot for one man, any man to take on. I want you to know that I know that."

"It's like this, captain. I don't *not* find my guy. The missing people case is one thing, but this whole string of murders? — it has my guts all out of whack, sir. There is something about all of this that just doesn't add up. There's murder and serial murders and domestic killings and this feels like none of those things."

"I feel that a little too, John. But, John, we'll get this guy, I know we will. I got my best man on the case and there is no fucking way he's going to let this guy slide. Take advantage of these federal resources, John. If this case is bigger than you or I then we're going to need the help."

"Thank you, Sir."

Shortly after my conversation with the captain, the two agents ask to see the bodies. I will spare the details of going to see the bodies with these two special agents. Just picture any cop show where this happens, and you'll have it pretty much nailed. Of course, Annie and I are probably a lot more fun than TV cops Bayliss and Cox and also a lot less whiney.

After visiting Annie in the morgue, we head to each crime scene, and I give them a thorough tour. Once that's over and I make sure *they know everything I know,* they'll get on with their business, and I'll get on with mine. They have their methods and their process and the ability to expedite a variety of technical needs that utilize a federal database and big taxpayer dollars. I have my instincts and my gut and my old beat. I have houses with doors that I can knock. Behind those doors are real people who just might talk.

"Agents, huh?" Annie says. "I wonder if the spend their time around a brick oven on a ninety-degree day?"

"Still going there, hey?"

"Yep."

The Feds

The next day, after the feds had thoroughly gone through my case files, the pair of them came to the very hasty conclusion that the bricks in the backyard of the house on the city's west side were the murder weapons. They were convinced that the owner of the house, Kameron Johnson, would be a primary suspect. They decided with federal authority that we would bring this man in for questioning.

All of these plans had been decided before I even stepped foot into One Monroe. These federal agents liked the hunt just as much as me. Unfortunately, I would compare them more to a poacher than a native — in this respect, the times haven't changed — maybe.

When I started my career as a cop, it was pagers that kept us on our toes. All those jag-offs throwing 911s through the airwaves while slamming a Taco Boy wet burrito. Easy enough to spot a dealer from a poser back then. Same with the cars. The way they'd pimp 'em out separated the boys from the big boys. Back then, I could drive up or down Division Avenue and bust just about anyone out walking after 9 pm. There were prostitutes all up and down the street—dealers and pimps rolled around with their 30-inch spoked wheels. There was also still a small gay block that was rife with Freddy Mercury mustaches, chaps, and those "Wild One" biker hats. There was a very clear line that separated wide-open delinquency from delinquency kept at bay — yes, I'm talking about those so holy as to not sin lest it be behind closed doors. I'm not sure if this was a simpler time, though. I think this was a result of some of the first rounds of gentrification. Let them have the city and we'll move out to the suburbs with the malls and restaurant chains and new construction. Now, folks are still doing this but also want their city back — all that Christmas charm that was depicted in all those old movies — window shopping amongst the backdrop of old six-story buildings. All this grime and grit is now pushed out and sheltered in place in the very first suburbs that the holy types moved out of in favor of even newer construction near those new outlet malls. Somehow, between here and there, the delinquents lost some of their swagger and became a little less hip. Oh sure, you still catch bits and pieces of that swagger in these old dandies who get all dressed up just to walk to the liquor store — even in 90-degree heat.

So, these agents have it in for the brick guy. They pegged him as both a dandy and a delinquent. Same ol' FBI with the same old suits and the same old boxy swagger. Kam Johnson has the motive — his son was killed after he fell out of work and his wife left him for a Protestant, a preacher nonetheless, and Kam had become a Muslim. All of this made him ripe for killing ol' whitey with a brick. "Not so fast," I say, "I have a feeling he's not our man!"

"We think he's our man, Mr. Rainey. We are bringing him in for questioning."

"I thought this was my case?"

"It is your case, you can thank us when we get our confession."

And so, no less than a swat team and these two agents take to the streets to bust in Johnson's door. They inched around the house, following a protocol as indicated by their training, and they eventually found Johnson in his basement, working on a small figurine of what appeared to be Malcolm X. The figurine had little tiny black glasses — their frames only partially painted. Johnson darted a little as though he might run, but quickly reconsidered. He put his hands gently up into the air. He was wearing a rust-orange cardigan and pleated pants. Watching them arrest him was like watching the arrest of Mr. Rogers.

"I'm unarmed… I'm unarmed… Don't shoot," Johnson said calmly but with a quiver. It was almost as though he'd rehearsed this moment over and over again. The scene was exactly how it should be.

"Kameron Johnson, you are under arrest for multiple homicides—"

"Multiple homicides?"

"Mr. Johnson, we are going to read you your rights."

"Ya'll know that I don't have no rights."

"Sir, you have the right to remain silent…"

And so, they arrested Kameron Johnson for serial homicide. If he could not afford an attorney, one would be provided to him by the state of Michigan and the United States of America.

As they removed Mr. Johnson from his home, the media was waiting outside with their cameras at the ready. The cops didn't shoot him, so the media would. Johnson nervously and innocently looked into the cameras and around the rest of the scene. He looked like a man who had no idea why we were there. "He's not our man — I know it." I look at Annie who is standing beside the captain and near both agents. I can see in her face that she agrees with me. The agents have no expression at all. I don't know how, but I'll be damned if I'm calling it case closed. We have barely touched the surface on this one.

Interrogation

Agents one and two stand quietly adjacent the captain and me. Mr. Johnson sits in interrogation room one waiting for whatever is coming his way. Whatever it was, it was coming with standard bureau questions from generic agent one and generic agent two. Questions like, "Where were you the night of…" and "…tell us about the bricks." Because of this, I'll spare you the first hour of questioning from dull and duller and skip ahead. From my point of view, you can see that Kameron Johnson is tired and frustrated. He has a calm and quiet patience that Hollywood might cast Lennie James in the role of. Similar voice too.

"Look, I know you all think that just because I have these bricks in my yard that it somehow makes me your guy. Having these bricks, bricks that have sat next to my garage for several years, anybody could have gotten their hands on them. An-y-one. You, you keep pressing me. No, I don't have an alibi, I barely leave the house. I'm tired and want to go home."

His likeness to Lennie James made it easy to feel compassion for him. He is tired and you can see it on him. I'm compelled to bring him a coffee and nudge at the questioning. And so, I open the door to the small room.

"I remember you," Kameron Johnson was looking sadly at the table when he said this. He then slowly lifted his head and looked me directly in the eyes. "You came to our house — you came to tell us that our son had been killed."

I place the coffee in front of him and he looks at it and back at me. "You remember? Of course you do. I can't imagine any man could forget such a thing. When I let myself, I remember it as though it was yesterday. I remember opening the door and seeing you standing there. I remember thinking you were a politician or a utility salesman. I remember you looking me in the eye and I knew — I knew right then — why you were there. The next moments are a little blurry — a lot blurry. I remember the look on Nalla's face before, and while, she collapsed to the floor. I remember thanking you for letting us know as I tended to her. Maybe it didn't go like that but, I'm not always sure. Like I said, it gets blurry, but yes, I remember you."

"Detective," Agent Mullins says, "I think it would be best if you—"

I raise my hand toward Agent Mullins and squat

down opposite Johnson. Whispering loudly I say, "Johnson, you need to think… do you have anything, I mean anything, that puts you anywhere other than the murder scenes — anything at all?"

"I was home, Detective. I'm always home. I've been home since my son died and Nalla left. I have never found a reason to go out in the world. Believe me, detective, I've tried."

"And the match on those bricks, Johnson. Can't you give me anything?"

"I am afraid not Detective. You all can't put this on me because of some old pile of bricks. You can't."

"Mr. Rainey."

"It's 'Detective' Rainey, Agent Mullens."

"Detective Rainey, we need to continue our line of questioning. I'd like to ask you to please exit the room for the time being."

I give Johnson one last look before glancing up at the agents and leaving the room. I'm no good here. I need to be out there — hunting down evidence.

August

The climate has changed. Nearly a month since they brought Kam Johnson in, and I still don't have any solid leads. There's still a mad tension in the air from all the political unrest. Last week in Atlanta, an officer, Officer Ben Shurrman, shot a man who fled from a speeding ticket — all while the fat cat old man talked about our walls and our borders. Tent cities became statements, while news dropped of a mass shooting in Arizona. So, I haven't been sleeping much, hence the lack of noir dreams. I did catch a glimpse of our dame last night while resting my eyes on the couch. She stood in the parking garage a few hundred feet from me. She took a bandana out of her pocket and tied it around her head — a blindfold. She reached into a duffle bag and pulled out a bottle with a rag hanging out of it. She looked at me and lit the rag before letting it drop to the concrete floor. Flames encompassed her and everything else in the room while I could only stand there, watching. I felt a hand on my shoulder. I turned to find Victoria behind me. She took my badge, wrapped it with a black ribbon, and whispered, "I got your back, detective," into my ear. I woke to the sound of the cat scratching at my front door.

Time for my morning run.

It takes me 45 minutes to run my routine 5-mile route. I'm on this curved stretch of road where city homes meet suburban landscapes. I always wonder how many times a guy like me was hit on this curve. This little stretch of east-to-west or west-to-east, sun-in-your-face, and blind ambition challenges both the pedestrian and the driver. No bike or walk lane, and an eighth of a mile with a split-second reaction time. No reaction time today — while I run, the brick killer runs with me. The Brick Killer. That first brick weighed in at 4.85 pounds. In a pallet, a quarter ton of bricks — 113 standard bricks — 113 murders. Brick-red blood in the streets of an uprising, and it's up to my knees. The foundation pavers of early America become the symbol of civil unrest. No way these old boys were killed by this quiet black man. No way this is about a son and vengeance. This is a different kind of war — a psychological "fuck you" to America.

Arriving home, I flick on the news while cooling down. A man named David Green is being interviewed regarding the murders. He has a Sig P365 holstered to his belt while giving the interview.

"I gotta keep me and my family safe, is all. Can't do nothin' about any of it but protect my right to bear arms and my right to protect my family. Sumpin' happens, well, I hate to say it, but they had it coming."

"Mr. Green, you say 'they,' but are you referring to Kam Johnson?"

"I said what I said."

"Live from the Kent County Courthouse, I'm Rachel O'Brien."

So, just like that — they had it coming. I swear I recognized the boys standing behind Green as the ones who were picking a fight with Jesse on the 4th. Then I get the call from downtown. One of ours got into a chase after a traffic violation. The whole thing escalated, and the officer needed to use deadly force. I'm told there's a cell phone video, and it's hitting the internet. The Captain says it doesn't look good — that it looks like an execution. He wants me to check out the footage and the scene. I tell him I don't have time right now, and he says that I do. I'm spiraling. I need my coffee. I open the door to my coke and the cat and head for the Bonneville. It's a Bonneville kind of day.

Parade Route

The drive to the scene of the officer-involved shooting is delayed by a rally of protesters marching in the park and on the sidewalks and on the road. It took almost no time for this group to form. They, there is that word, marched and chanted and multiplied as I drove slowly through the crowd; glad I drove the Bonneville. The air smells like thirteen different types of smoke and officers are starting to appear in and around the groups. It's the bicycle brigade. Near the courthouse, that man Green from the news is standing with a rather large group of what appear to be NRA members with their colorful sidearms and semi-automatic rifles. The whole place is a tinderbox — a Molotov cocktail. I hope nobody brought matches to this thing.

Then I see her.

She's wearing an army field jacket and slacks, her hair in cornrows. It's not just that I see her rather, she sees me and is looking into me. She lowers her megaphone to her hip — she barely has a grip on it. As my car inches forward, we are staring at each other. The entire time felt as though it was in slow motion while with the same frame-by-

fame progress her eyes squint. I'm startled when
the car behind me honks its horn alerting me to the
fact that there is a solid car-length gap between
me and the car in front of me. The woman raises her
megaphone and in my direction yells,

"Defund the police."

I recognize her. Nalla.

Green Apples

After leaving the scene of the officer-involved fatal, I made a call and got the address of this Green fellow. I drove out of the city and into the fields, then pulled into his long dirt driveway, up to a house surrounded by dirt paths, old cars, and a barn. As I let myself out to look around, Mr. Green and the boys from the news appeared, seemingly from out of nowhere, with their firearms.

"Can we help you?" Green asked.

"Sir, my name is Detective John Rainey, and I—"

"I'm sorry, did you say detective? Let me see your ID and a warrant, or you best be on your way."

"Sir—"

"I'm still waiting for that warrant," he said as he placed his hand near his firearm."

"Are you threatening an officer?"

"No, sir. I know my rights and am making sure you know them, too."

"It's 'Detective.'"

I noticed that just off to the side of the car, the same Monte Carlo that these boys had left the bar in on the Fourth of July, sitting in the dirt, was a single brick. I had the feeling you get when you can smell your prey inching toward your bait.

"Mr. Green—"

"Detective, why don't you get back in your car and be on your way? I'm sure you have no reason to be trespassing here."

I was sure I had a pile of reasons.

Bricks

It was mid-June, about two weeks before the first Brick Murder. Dave Green took a break from his Coors Light to answer the phone. A man's voice, disguised and garbled yet deep, conveyed seriousness in tone and nature.

"Mr. Green, I have a request from the top — a request of the utmost importance."

Dave's hands trembled as he tried to remove the lit cigarette from his mouth, the cigarette sticking to his lips. His voice shook as he responded, "Yes, sir, whatever you need."

"I need you to start a war for us all, Mr. Green. This patriotic gesture will be remembered in history. However, this duty must remain secret. Are you capable of such patriotism, Mr. Green?"

"Me, sir?"

"Yes, Mr. Green. We need you to start a war."

"A war, sir?"

"Mr. Green, you'll find in your possession a stash of bricks and your instructions. You'll complete the job, won't you? An A-plus job?"

"Yes, sir. Whatever you need, sir. A-plus."

About The Author

Aaron Paul Schaut's dad always said that when Aaron was born, he wanted him to have a good name. So, he gave him the pen name, or musician's name, Aaron Paul. Since Aaron wouldn't start using this name until 2023, it turns out that some other guy was already using the name Aaron Paul. So, it's Aaron Paul Schaut, yo.

Aaron Paul Schaut has independently published three books under the "These Americans" banner. He was also featured in Starlite Pulp Review #3 with his short story, "The Depression of John Stonebrook."

More to Discover

Check out the 'These Americans' series in its entirety from author Aaron Paul Schaut.

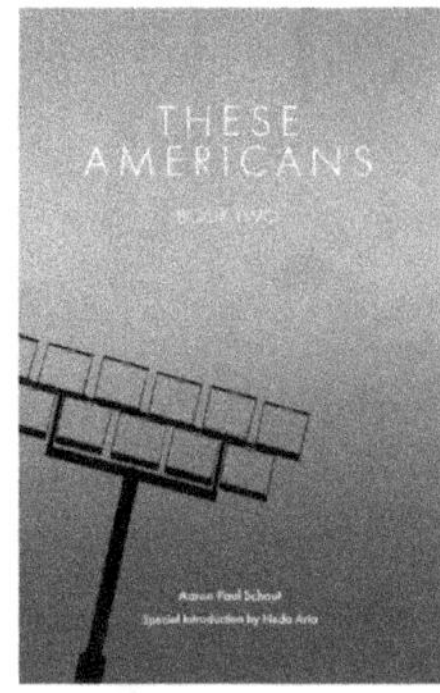

Dig into the books from Starlite Pulp — Dig into all of them.

Visit aaronschaut.com for more.

www.ingramcontent.com/pod-product-compliance
Lightning Source LLC
Chambersburg PA
CBHW060505300726
48975CB00008B/2651